Mr. Kugsley's
Very Interesting
Monster Science

"What have you invented?" you ask politely.

"This is my latest," he says.

He reaches into a jar and takes out a handful of powder. Then he tosses it at you.

"Achoo!" You sneeze. "Achoo! Achoo! Achoo!"

"Hooray!" the old man squeals. "It works! My invention works! I made you invisible!"

If you demand that Kugsley make you visible again, turn to page 24.

If you like the idea of being invisible, turn to page 26.

**WHAT WILL HAPPEN NEXT?
TURN THE PAGE FOR
MORE THRILLS AND FUN!
WHATEVER YOU DO,
IT'S UP TO YOU!**

WHICH WAY SECRET DOOR Books for you to enjoy

#1   Wow! You Can Fly!
#2   Giants, Elves and Scary Monsters
#3   The Haunted Castle
#4   The Secret Life of Toys
#5   The Visitor from Outer Space
#6   The Inch-High Kid
#7   The Magic Carpet
#8   Happy Birthday to You
#9   The Monster Family
#10 Brontosaurus Moves In

Available from ARCHWAY paperbacks

which way · secret door · books

#9

R.G. Austin

The Monster Family

Illustrated by
Blanche Sims

AN ARCHWAY PAPERBACK
Published by POCKET BOOKS • NEW YORK

AN ARCHWAY PAPERBACK *Original*

An Archway Paperback published by
POCKET BOOKS, a division of Simon & Schuster, Inc.
1230 Avenue of the Americas, New York, N.Y. 10020

ISBN: 0-671-47570-3

First Archway Paperback printing January, 1984

10 9 8 7 6 5 4 3 2 1

AN ARCHWAY PAPERBACK and colophon are
trademarks of Simon & Schuster, Inc.

WHICH WAY is a registered trademark
of Simon & Schuster, Inc.

SECRET DOOR is a trademark
of Simon & Schuster, Inc.

Printed in the U.S.A.

IL   1+

For Terry and Rita,
my favorite collaborators

ATTENTION!

READING A SECRET DOOR BOOK IS LIKE PLAYING A GAME.

HERE ARE THE RULES

Begin reading on page 1. When you come to a choice, decide what to do and follow the directions. Keep reading and following the directions until you come to an ending. Then go back to the beginning and make new choices.

There are many stories and many endings in this book.

HAVE FUN!

It is dark outside. You have gone to bed, but you are still wide awake.

You lie quietly until everyone in the house is asleep. Then you creep out of bed and tiptoe into the closet.

You push away the clothes and knock three times on the back wall. Soon the secret door begins to move. It opens just wide enough for you to slip through.

Turn to page 2.

On the other side is a country road. In the middle of the road is a shiny silver bicycle. The license plate has your name on it.

You climb onto the bike and pedal away. Ssssssss.

"Oh, no!" You just rode over a piece of broken glass. You have a flat tire and no way to fix it!

"Hi," says a voice. "I'm Sam. Looks like you have a problem."

You turn and see a very weird-looking boy.

"I have a flat tire," you explain.

"That's no problem," says Sam. "We can fix it. I have all the stuff in my cellar. Come on."

You follow Sam into a big old house. His mother greets you at the door.

"Well, hello," she says. "My name is Juna. Why don't you come have a snack."

If you go with Juna to get a snack, turn to page 5.

If you go with Sam to the cellar, turn to page 6.

You walk with the woman into the kitchen. While she is fixing a snack, you look at the yard. It is very, very strange.

There are black birds everywhere. And toads. And there is a baby dragon swinging by his tail on a jungle gym.

"Here's your snack," Juna says with a smile. "Grasshopper sandwiches and mushroom juice. They're Sam's favorites!"

If you don't think you can eat this snack, turn to page 34.

If you think you should be polite and eat the snack, turn to page 36.

You follow Sam down some
long rickety steps. A cobweb
sticks on your face.
"Yuck!" you say.
"Don't worry," says the boy.
"The spider is a friend of
mine. I keep telling him
not to build his web
there, but he's stub-
born."
*This kid is a little
strange,* you think.

Sam picks up a patch kit from the table.

"Now, where is that bicycle pump?" he says. "Last time I saw it, Bertha was playing with it."

Then Sam walks into another room.

If you follow Sam, turn to page 8.

If you stay where you are, turn to page 10.

Just as you walk through the door, you hear a strange noise.

"Whoosh! Shoosh!"

"Bertha! Stop that!" Sam says.

You cannot believe your eyes. Bertha is a raccoon. And she is squirting air from a bicycle pump right at a huge spider web. The web is shaking and shaking.

"Bertha just loves to torment those spiders," Sam explains. "Stop it, Bertha! Give me that pump."

Bertha makes a weird noise and races into the next room with the pump.

If you help Sam chase Bertha, turn to page 12.

If you check to see if the spiders are okay, turn to page 14.

As soon as Sam disappears, you hear footsteps. Then, suddenly, a funny-looking man, a dog, and a clatter of pots tumble down the stairs.

"Jeepers, creepers!" says a voice. "I'm always tripping over those pots!"

"Oops!" says the man when he sees you. "I thought I was alone. My name's Kugsley. What's yours?"

You introduce yourself and tell him about your flat tire.

"Well," says Kugsley, "it's real nice to have you here. We don't get much company. Come on. Let me show you my new invention."

If you go to see Kugsley's invention, turn to page 20.

If you do not want to go, turn to page 22.

You run after Sam, who is running after Bertha. The raccoon runs into the next room. You and Sam follow her.

"Groowrooooah!" You hear a terrible, awful roar. "Roooahhaar!"

You are face to face with a mini-dragon!

"Yikes!" you scream.

"Easy there, Agatha," Sam says to the dragon. "It's only me . . . I mean me and my friend."

"Whooosh! Shooosh!" Bertha is pumping air at Agatha.

"Come on, Bertha. Give me a break," Sam says. "You're a pest. Hand over the pump."

Bertha pumps air at Sam.

If you try to grab the pump from Bertha, turn to page 16.

If you try to trick Bertha, turn to page 18.

You look at the web.
An adult spider is standing
in the middle. She points
to the floor with one of
her legs.

*I must have imagined
that,* you think.

You look down. Baby
spiders are crawling all over
the floor looking for their home.
There is no way that they can get back
to the web by themselves.

I've got to help them, you think.

You get a piece of paper from a table. One by one, you pick up the baby spiders and put them on the paper. Then you put them all back in their web. As you leave the room to join Sam, you look back at the spiders.

You cannot be certain, but you think you see the mother spider wave at you.

The End

Just as you reach out to grab the pump, a slithery snake crawls right in front of you!

You jump back, and Bertha makes a run for it.

"Quick!" you yell to Sam. "Follow Bertha!"

But the dragon, determined to help her friend, blocks your way. Bertha escapes through a hole in the cellar wall.

"We'll never get the pump now," you wail. "And if I don't get home before dark, I'll really be in trouble."

You are so upset that you begin to cry. You do not notice the snake crawl close to you. You do not even see the snake when he curls up in a big circle just the size of your bicycle tire.

"Pssst!" says the snake. "Pssst!"

You look down and realize that he is offering to turn himself into a tire.

In no time at all, you have wrapped this wonderful new friend around your wheel.

And you manage, with the help of the snake, to get home before dark.

The End

The only thing you know about raccoons is that they love to eat.

"You know what?" you say very loudly to Sam. "I had the greatest dinner last night! And you should see all the leftovers. We have steak and baked potatoes and green beans and ice cream."

You look at Bertha. She is drooling!

"And, Sam," you say, "if I can just get home, I can share those leftovers with anybody I want. Isn't that great?"

In a flash, Bertha hands you the pump. Before you know it, your tire is fixed and you are on the way home.

Your new pet is riding on the handlebars.

The End

You and Kugsley climb up a long spiral staircase. The dog runs in front of you. When you get to the top, Kugsley opens the door. You are amazed! There are bottles and tubes everywhere.

"Is this a laboratory?" you ask.

"Yep," says Kugsley. "And it's all mine."

"Are you a scientist?"

"Sometimes," Kugsley says.

"What have you invented?" you ask politely.

"This is my latest," Kugsley says.

He reaches into a jar and takes out a handful of powder. Then he tosses it at you.

"Achoo!" you sneeze. "Achoo! Achoo! Achoo!"

"Hooray!" Kugsley squeals. "It works! My invention works!"

"What works? You made me sneeze. Big deal!" you say. "Pepper can make me do that."

"What do you mean, sneeze, kiddo?" says Kugsley. "I made you invisible! Watch this!"

He throws some powder on the dog. The dog disappears.

If you demand that Kugsley make you visible again, turn to page 24.

If you like the idea of being invisible, turn to page 27.

You wait for Sam. Soon he returns with the pump.

"I got it!" he says. "But I can't fix your tire right now. I have to go to a costume party. Do you want to come with me?"

"Sure, I'd love to go. Do I have to wear a costume?" you ask.

"That's up to you."

If you think you should wear a costume, turn to page 50.

If you go to the party without a costume, turn to page 53.

You look at your hand. Your hand is gone.

"I demand that you change me back right now!" you tell Kugsley in a loud voice.

"I don't know, kid. I'm not sure I have perfected the formula yet. But I'll give it a try."

Kugsley reaches into another jar and takes out a handful of red powder. He tosses it at you.

You feel yourself changing.

"Thank goodness!" you tell Kugsley. "Your powder works!"

"Yeah," he says. "I guess you can call that working."

He looks around the room.

"Here's a tire for your bike. Quick! I'll help you put it on."

Soon you are on the way home. You are so thankful that you are no longer invisible that you never even notice your pointed head!

The End

"Gee," you say to Kugsley. "I think being invisible could be fun."

"You're right," Kugsley says. "Let's go play some tricks."

Kugsley throws some powder on himself, and the two of you walk outside. Kugsley's dog goes with you.

Just then, you see the mailman coming up the path.

If you choose to play a trick on the neighbors, turn to page 28.

If you choose to play a trick on the mailman, turn to page 32.

You walk into the neighbors' house. A woman is watching TV. She is reaching for a glass of juice. A man is reading a newspaper.

"You take the juice," Kugsley whispers. "I'll take the newspaper."

You dash across the room and lift the glass of juice off the table.

"My stars!" the woman says as she reaches for the juice. "Barstow! Look at that! My juice is flying!"

"That's nice, dear," Barstow says, not bothering to look.

"Barstow!" the woman screams. "Do something this instant! My juice is flying!"

Quickly, you put the glass down on the table.

Barstow looks up and smiles. "It's your head that's flying, dear. Your juice is on the table."

"So it is," the woman says, shaking her head.

(continued on page 30)

The woman starts to watch TV again. Kugsley grabs the man's newspaper.

"Matilda!" the man says. "My newspaper is flying!"

"Yes, dear," Matilda says, without taking her eyes from the screen.

"Matilda! Look! It's flying around the room!"

"Ghosts! Matilda! We have ghosts in the house!"

"What, dear?"

"Ghosts," the man says.

"Don't be silly," Matilda says.

Barstow looks at the TV for a moment. Kugsley puts the paper in Barstow's lap.

When the man notices the newspaper, he scratches his head. "Matilda, I think we both better go get our eyes checked."

You and Kugsley walk out laughing.

The End

Kugsley shoves the dog right in the mail-man's path.

"Grrrrr," growls the dog.

The mailman looks around for the dog, but he does not see anything.

"Grrrr, Grrrrr, Grrrr." The dog growls even louder. Then it grabs the mailman's pant leg.

"Hey!" yells the mailman, shaking his leg. "What is this? What's happening to me?"

The mailman falls down and his letters go flying. He is very confused.

Quickly, Kugsley picks up the dog. And, while the mailman is still scratching his head, you pick up all the letters and put them back in the bag.

"I don't know . . ." the mailman says. "I guess this just isn't my day!"

The End

"I think I'll just go out and play," you say as politely as you can.

"All right, dear," Juna says. "Just be careful about Agatha. She's the dragon."

As soon as you step out the door, big black birds fly around your head. Yuck. They are all over you.

You swing your hands at the birds.

Just then, Sam comes out of the house to tell you he has fixed your bicycle tire. He sees you swinging your hands at the birds.

"Don't do that!" he screams. "Agatha loves those birds. You'll make her angry."

But the warning is too late. Agatha starts running toward you. Smoke is shooting from her mouth.

If you make a run for it, turn to page 38.

If you scream at Agatha, turn to page 40.

I have always been taught not to hurt people's feelings, you think. But goodness! I wonder what will happen if I actually eat this mess!

If you think that you can pretend to eat the sandwich, turn to page 54.

If you don't think you can fake it, turn to page 55.

You run toward the house. Agatha runs after you. And Sam runs after both of you!

You race through the kitchen door and down the hall to the front door.

You run through the door. Your bike is standing right outside. You look back. Agatha is coming out the door!

You hop on your bike and pedal as fast as you can.

You feel Agatha's hot breath right behind you. And you hear Sam.

"Stop, Agatha. Stop!" he yells.

You pedal *even* faster.

After five minutes, you look back. Agatha has given up the chase.

You stop your bike and wave good-bye to Sam.

"Come back another day," Sam yells.

"Sure," you say. *Fat chance,* you think.

The End

Agatha is coming right at you!

"Stop!" you yell.

Agatha looks startled.

"I said stop!" you yell even louder. "You're being a bully!"

Agatha shakes her head.

"Yes, you are. Now, if you want to make this even, stop chasing me and let's have a race."

Agatha nods her head.

"Now, this is what we are going to do," you say. "We'll run around the yard three times. The first one to get to that big plant over there in the garden is the winner."

You and Agatha line up.

"Ready! Set! Go!" yells Sam.

If you want to win the race, turn to page 42.

If you want to lose the race, turn to page 44.

You're off! You run as fast as you can! Around the yard one time. Two times! Three times!

You glance behind you. You are winning! You run toward the huge strange-looking plant in the garden.

You reach the plant and touch it. "I won!" you yell. "I won!"

You turn to look at Agatha. She does not look sad. She looks scared.

What is she scared of? you think. *I can't imagine what it could be.*

Suddenly, you look at the plant. It is a gigantic Venus flytrap!

If you don't know what a Venus flytrap is, turn to page 47.

If you know what a Venus flytrap is, turn to page 48.

You do not think it would be smart to beat Agatha in a race. After all, a dragon who loses a race might get pretty angry! And an angry dragon might be a very sore loser!

The dragon races ahead of you. When she reaches the finish line, she wags her tail. She is very excited that she won.

I bet she never won a race before, you think. *After all, dragons aren't very fast creatures.*

Agatha is so thrilled that she plays with you for the rest of the afternoon. You have a terrific time. And when it is time to go home, you give her a big hug.

I never knew losing could be so much fun, you think.

The End

A Venus flytrap is an insectivorous plant. That means that it is a plant that eats insects such as flies and gnats.

It has leaves that open and close with sharp spines along the edges. When an insect touches the leaf, it opens and then closes on the insect.

The Venus flytrap in the monster family's garden is gigantic. It is even bigger than you are. It is big enough to eat you.

You have just touched this gigantic Venus flytrap.

LOOK OUT!

The End

It is a good thing you know what a Venus flytrap is. Because this one is gigantic. It is even bigger than you are!

Uh-oh, you think. *That must be what Agatha is afraid of!*

You look at the plant. Its mouth is starting to open.

"Yikes!" you scream. And you jump back just in time.

You are lucky you know what a Venus flytrap is!

The End

Sam gives you a mustache and a beard and a pointed hat. Then you and Sam go to the party.

There is a prize for the person who can do the best trick.

Some people pull rabbits out of hats. Others make things disappear. All you can do is a somersault.

When it is your turn, you take off your hat and do somersaults all over the room.

Everybody screams and claps and cheers when they see your somersaults. They have never seen such an amazing thing!

People with pointed heads can't do somersaults!

Naturally, you win the prize.

The End

When you get to the party, you are embarrassed that you are not wearing a costume. You really want to go home. But you know that you have to be a good sport and not spoil the party for Sam. So you stay.

When they have the contest for the best costume, you want to run away and hide. But you stay.

And you know what? You win the contest. None of the monsters could figure out how you made your head round instead of pointed!

Your prize is a pet bat of your very own. You hope your mother will be a good sport.

The End

54

"I think I'll just have a half a sandwich," you tell Juna as politely as you can. "I'm not very hungry right now."

"Sure," she says sweetly. "I understand." *Well, here goes,* you think.

Turn to page 56.

I will be very brave, you think. *I will close my eyes and pretend they are not grasshoppers at all. I'll pretend they are French fries.*

Your stomach growls as you open your mouth. You feel like throwing up. The grasshoppers crunch in your teeth.

Just as you take your second bite, Juna says, "Oh, by the way. There aren't really grasshoppers in that sandwich. It's just lettuce rolled up in balls. Sam calls them grasshoppers because they're so green and crunchy."

Whew! you think. *That was a close call!*

The End

But before you take a bite, you have an idea!

You take all the green grasshoppers from your half of the sandwich and put them in the other half. Then you eat the bread.

That was clever of me, you think.

"Mmm," you tell Juna. "That was delicious."

"Well," says Juna as she hands you a glass of brownish liquid. "If you liked that, you are going to love this slug juice. It's my specialty."

The End